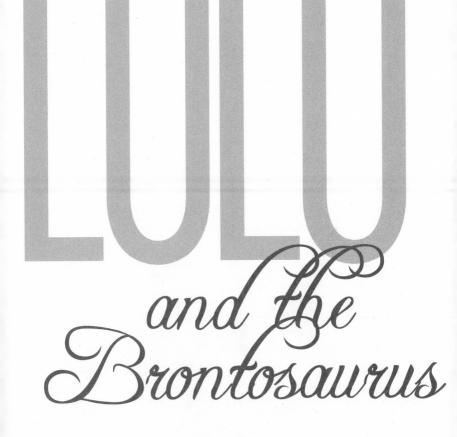

LULU
and the
Brontosaurus

JUDITH VIORST

illustrated by LANE SMITH

Atheneum Books for Young Readers

NEW YORK · LONDON · TORONTO · SYDNEY · NEW DELHI

ATHENEUM BOOKS FOR YOUNG READERS
An imprint of Simon & Schuster Children's Publishing Division
1230 Avenue of the Americas, New York, New York 10020

ATHENEUM BOOKS FOR YOUNG READERS is a registered trademark of Simon & Schuster, Inc.

For information about special discounts for bulk purchases, please contact Simon & Schuster
Special Sales at 1-866-506-1949 or business@simonandschuster.com.

The Simon & Schuster Speakers Bureau can bring authors to your live event.
For more information or to book an event, contact the Simon & Schuster Speakers Bureau at
1-866-248-3049 or visit our website at www.simonspeakers.com.

Also available in an Atheneum Books for Young Readers hardcover edition.

The text for this book is set in Officina Sans.

The illustrations for this book are rendered in pencil on pastel paper.

Manufactured in the United States of America

0317 FFG

First Atheneum Books for Young Readers paperback edition April 2012

10 9

The Library of Congress has cataloged the hardcover edition as follows:
Viorst, Judith.
Lulu and the brontosaurus / Judith Viorst ; illustrated by Lane Smith.
p. cm.
Summary: Lulu's parents refuse to give in when she demands a brontosaurus for her
birthday and so she sets out to find her own, but while the brontosaurus she finally
meets approves of pets, he does not intend to be Lulu's.
ISBN 978-1-4169-9961-4 (hardcover)
[1. Behavior—Fiction. 2. Apatosaurus—Fiction. 3. Pets—Fiction. 4. Birthdays—Fiction.]
I. Smith, Lane, ill. II. Title.
PZ7.V816Lul 2010
[Fic]—dc22
2009031664
ISBN 978-1-4169-9962-1 (pbk)
ISBN 978-1-4169-9963-8 (eBook)

BOOK DESIGN BY MOLLY LEACH

For Nathaniel Redding Gwadz Viorst
and Benjamin Carlo Gwadz Viorst,
who helped me write this story
—J. V.

For Molly
—L. S.

OKAY! *All right! You don'*

I know that people and dinosaurs have never lived on Earth at the same time. And *I know* that dinosaurs aren't living now. I even also know that paleontologists (folks who study dinosaurs) decided that a dinosaur that was once called a brontosaurus (a very nice name) shouldn't be called brontosaurus anymore, and

have to tell me! I know!

---

changed it to apatosaurus
(a kind of ugly name). But since
I'm the person writing this story,
I get to choose what I write, and
I'm writing about a girl and a
B R O N T O S A U R U S.
So if you don't want to read this
book, you can close it up right
now—you won't hurt my
feelings. And if you still want
to read it, here goes:

chapter one

There once was a girl named Lulu, and she was a pain. She wasn't a pain in the elbow. She wasn't a pain in the knee. She was a pain—a very big pain—in the

b u t t .

Now, Lulu was an only child, and her mom and her dad gave her everything she wanted. And guess what? Lulu wanted EVERYTHING. Tons of candy. Tons of toys. Tons of watching tons of cartoons on TV. And if her mom and her dad ever said (and they hardly ever said it), "Sorry, darling, we think you've had enough," Lulu would screech till the lightbulbs burst and throw herself down on the floor, and then she would kick her heels and wave her arms. And pretty soon her mom and her dad would say, "Well, just this once," and let her have whatever it was she wanted.

chapter two

Two weeks before Lulu's birthday, she announced to her mom and her dad that she wanted a brontosaurus for her b-day present. What did she say? What? A brontosaurus? Yes, she wanted a brontosaurus for a pet. At first Lulu's mom and her dad just thought she was making a little joke. And then they saw— oh, horrors!—that she was serious.

They patiently explained that a brontosaurus is a quite enormous dinosaur who lives in forests, not in people's houses.

(Is that where a brontosaurus would live? In a forest? I'm afraid that I'm not absolutely sure. But since I'm the person writing this story, I'm putting this brontosaurus in a forest, along with a lot of other wild beasts that I'm absolutely sure did not live on Earth when dinosaurs were there.)

Anyway, Lulu's mom and her dad continued explaining to her, although a brontosaurus is into eating plants, not animals (including human animals like Lulu), and although it is cute (in a long-necked, pinheaded way), it is much too huge and too wild to be a good pet.

A dog,
a cat,
a goldfish,
a bird,
a gerbil,
a guinea pig, yes.

A brontosaurus?

Definitely no.

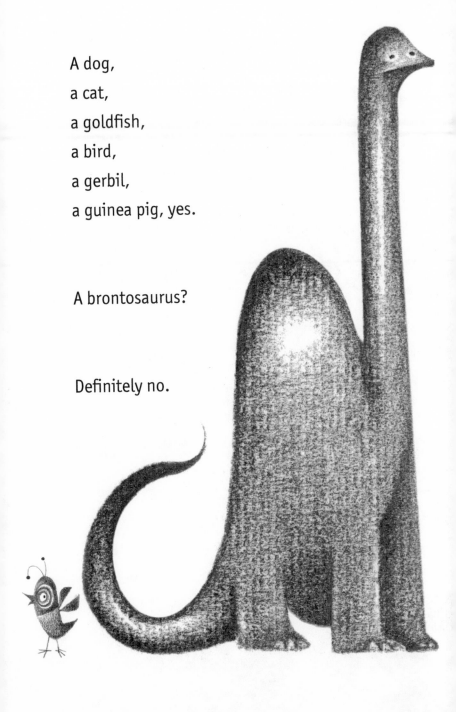

chapter three

No? Her mom and her dad were telling Lulu no? Lulu wasn't used to hearing no. And she hated—she really hated—hearing no. To show how much she hated it, she screeched and screeched and screeched till all the lightbulbs in the living room burst.

"I WANT A BRONTOSAURUS FOR MY BIRTHDAY PRESENT," she said in between screeches.

"I WANT A BRONTOSAURUS FOR A PET."

"Well, maybe we could get you a nice pet rabbit," said her mom.

"Or even," said her dad, "a nice pet rat."

"Nononononononono!" screeched Lulu.

"I WANT A BRONTOSAURUS FOR A PET."

Then she threw herself down on the floor and kicked her heels and waved her arms and screeched some more.

chapter four

Four days, eight days, ten days, twelve days passed. Lulu kept saying, "I WANT A BRONTOSAURUS." Her mom and her dad just kept on saying no. Lulu kept screeching and throwing herself on the floor and kicking her heels and waving her arms. Lulu's mom and her dad kept saying no. Until finally, on the thirteenth day, the day before Lulu's birthday, right after lunch, Lulu said to her mom and her dad, "Okay then, foo on you." (She had terrible manners.) "If you aren't going to get me a brontosaurus, I'm going out and getting one for myself."

Lulu packed a small suitcase, said good-bye to her mom and her dad, and walked out the door.

And they let her go! Partly because they thought she'd change her mind and come running back home in about two minutes. And partly because it was nice to not have her screeching and kicking and waving and being a pain.

"Let's have a cup of tea and a couple of cookies," Lulu's mom said to her dad.

"Excellent idea," her dad replied.

So they went into the kitchen and started munching on some cookies and sipping tea. And pretty soon they'd forgotten all about Lulu.

chapter five

But Lulu hadn't forgotten that she was going to get herself a brontosaurus. And luckily for Lulu, there was a great big forest not too far from her house. The animals in that forest had never bothered anybody, because nobody had ever bothered them. But—watch out, creatures!— here came Lulu, trudging through the forest, swinging her small suitcase back and forth, and—in a quite loud voice that was sure to wake the napping animals from their naps—singing this song:

I'm gonna, I'm gonna, I'm gonna

gonna get

A bronto-bronto-bronto
Brontosaurus for a pet.

I'm gonna, I'm gonna,
I'm gonna, gonna get

A bronto-bronto-bronto
Brontosaurus for a pet.

The forest that Lulu was trudging through was overgrown with trees whose branches scratched her face and whose roots she tripped over. But Lulu hardly noticed, because she was thinking just one thought, and you know what that was.

So on she went, swinging her suitcase and singing her song too loud and annoying all the creatures in the forest, and being the same big pain out there that she was back home in her house,

until . . .

Slithering down from the branch of a
tree came a long, fat, brown-black snake,
who had been peacefully snoozing till
Lulu woke him up. Sleepy and grumpy
and hissing an exceedingly nasty hiss,
he wrapped himself around Lulu, around
and around and tighter and tighter, and
told her she'd really be sorry that she had
awakened him.

"I'm going to squeeze you dead," he said.

(Okay, so snakes don't talk. But in my story they do.)

And Lulu said, "Not if I squeeze you deader."

So Lulu squeezed the snake—hard!— and the snake yelled, "Ow!" and quickly unwrapped himself from Lulu. And Lulu, wiping some snake sweat from the palms of her snake-squeezing hands, went on trudging deeper into the forest.

chapter six

I'm gonna, I'm gonna,
  I'm gonna, gonna get
A bronto-bronto-bronto
  Brontosaurus for a pet.
I'm gonna, I'm gonna,
  I'm gonna, gonna get
A bronto-bronto-bronto
  Brontosaurus for a pet.

Singing her brontosaurus song in a louder and louder voice, Lulu was waking up nappers all over the forest. Some were annoyed. Some were extremely annoyed. Among the extremely annoyed was a silky, slinky lady tiger, who yawned and stretched and rubbed her bright green eyes, and then, with a ferocious roar, sprung out from behind some trees and pounced on Lulu.

"You're a big pain," the tiger said, "so I'm going to eat you up for my afternoon snack."

"Uh-uh," said Lulu. "I'm bonking you on the head." And swinging, swinging with all her might, Lulu bonked the tiger with her suitcase.

The tiger yelled, "Ow!" and fell down in a pitiful black-and-orange-striped heap on the forest floor. Lulu brushed off a few tiger hairs that were stuck to the side of her tiger-bonking suitcase and went on trudging deeper into the forest.

chapter seven

As the afternoon turned into late afternoon and then into early evening, Lulu trudged ever deeper into the forest. When she felt hungry, she opened her suitcase and took out a pickle sandwich.

When she felt cold, she took out a
sweater and socks. And when it got
buggy, she opened her suitcase and
took out some bug spray and sprayed.
She was feeling a little tired, but she
kept trudging, and swinging her suitcase,
and singing her song.

I'm gonna, I'm gonna,
I'm gonna, gonna get
A bronto-bronto-bronto
Brontosaurus for a pet.
I'm gonna, I'm gonna,
I'm gonna, gonna get
A bronto-bronto-bronto
Brontosaurus for a pet.

Now, a big black bear who liked listening to the music that insects make in the early evening couldn't hear their song because Lulu's was louder. Plus, a lot of the insects were deader because Lulu kept on spraying them with her spray. This made him mad. Then madder. Then madder than that. He growled a thunderous growl, and then he lumbered heavily down the forest path and stood on his two hind legs in front of Lulu. Waving a big claw-y paw in her face, he said, "You're interrupting my favorite program." (Please don't give me an argument. In my story, bears are allowed to have favorite programs.) "So I'm going to scratch you to pieces with my claws."

Lulu glared at the big black bear and put her hands on her hips. "Nobody's scratching me," she told the bear. Then she jumped—as high as she possibly could—in the air. Then she landed—as hard as she possibly could—on his foot.

The bear yelled, "Ow!" and went limping away, as fast as a bear could limp with one stomped foot. And after shaking some broken bear toenails off the bottoms of her bear-stomping shoes, Lulu went trudging deeper into the forest.

chapter eight

Lulu was now in the deepest, darkest, quietest part of the forest. It was getting quite late and she was getting quite tired. She took her sleeping bag out of her suitcase, spread it on the ground, and lay down to sleep. But before she slept, she sang her song once more.

I'm gonna, I'm gonna,
I'm gonna, gonna get
A bronto-bronto-bronto
Brontosaurus for a pet.
I'm gonna, I'm gonna,
I'm gonna, gonna get
A bronto-bronto-bronto
Brontosaurus for a pet.

Actually, she never even got to sing
the last line because, before she could
get to it, she was sleeping.

chapter eight
and one half

At dawn Lulu woke to the sound of birds calling to one another, and the dusky-musky smell of the forest floor, and the feel of a gentle late-summer breeze blowing across her face, and the taste (because she hadn't bothered to brush her teeth before bedtime) of yesterday's pickle sandwich. She also woke to the sight of something so huge, so enormous, so utterly gigantic that she thought—no, she was sure—that she was still dreaming. It looked like a mountain, except this mountain had legs, a very long neck, and a very small head. It was (as I'm sure you've already figured out) the brontosaurus that Lulu had been searching for.

chapter nine

Lulu closed, then opened, then closed, then opened her eyes again, and decided she wasn't dreaming after all. She quickly climbed out of her sleeping bag and announced to the brontosaurus, "It's my birthday today and—just in time!—I've found you."

"No, *I've* found *you*," the brontosaurus told Lulu. "And I'd like to wish you a very happy birthday."

"Oh, it will be very happy," Lulu said
to the brontosaurus, "because you"—she
patted his ankle, because his ankle was
as high as she could reach—"you
are the pet I'm getting for my birthday."

The brontosaurus bent down his
neck so his face was close to Lulu's.
He looked at her back to front and head
to toes, sniffing at her carefully with
his brontosaurus nose and making a
rumbling noise (nobody knows how
dinosaurs sound, but in my story they
rumble) and slowly nodding, nodding
his pinheaded head.

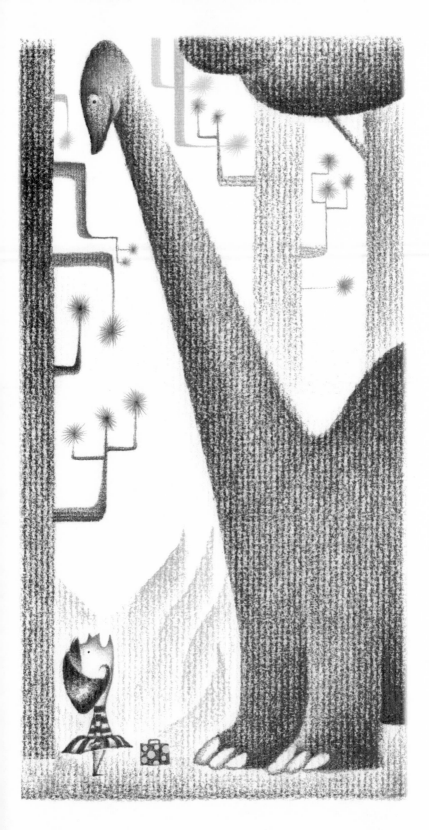

"A pet," he said to Lulu, after he'd nodded for a while, "is a very good thing."

"A very, very good thing," Lulu replied. She opened up her suitcase and went digging around inside and pulled out a white leather collar, which she fastened around the brontosaurus's neck.

"Now I'll just attach this leash"—she dug some more and found a long, long leash in her suitcase—"and take you home with me."

Lulu attached the leash to the collar, feeling so pleased with herself that she sang a whole new brontosaurus song.

I got it! I got it! I got
What I wanted to get,
A bronto-bronto-bronto
Brontosaurus for a pet.
I got it! I got it! I got
What I wanted to get,
A bronto-bronto-bronto
Brontosaurus for a pet.

She would have kept feeling pleased
with herself, except now the brontosaurus
was shaking his head. And now, in his
rumbling voice, he was saying, "No." He
was saying no and shaking his head till
the collar and leash flew off. "No," he
said, "I don't wish to be your pet."

Lulu, remember, hated hearing no. She
really, really hated hearing no. So she
screeched till all the birds fled from the
trees, and then she threw herself down on
the forest floor, and then she kicked her
heels and waved her arms.

The brontosaurus waited patiently, without saying one more word, until she had stopped with the screeching and kicking and waving. "Finished now?" he quite politely asked.

"Maybe I am," Lulu said. "And maybe I'm not. It all depends"—and here she shook a finger right in the brontosaurus's face; this girl was a pain, but she wasn't a scaredy-cat— "it all depends on whether you stop saying no and start saying yes to being my pet."

The brontosaurus shook his head no some more. Lulu thought about screeching and so forth some more. But instead she said, in a very snippy voice, "Now listen here, you were the one who said to me just a minute ago that—and I quote—'A PET IS A VERY GOOD THING.'"

"That's what I said," the brontosaurus admitted.

"So what," Lulu asked, "is your problem, Mr. B?"

"No problem," he answered. "Just a misunderstanding. Because when I said that a pet is a very good thing, I didn't mean I wanted to be *your* pet. I meant that *you'd* be a very good pet for *me*."

chapter ten

Lulu's eyes were two round Os of amazement. She tried to speak, but at first no words came out. Then finally she was able to say, in a squeaky, amazed kind of voice, "I don't think I heard what I think I just heard, Mr. B."

"You did indeed," the brontosaurus replied.

"Well, if I did"—Lulu's voice was back to being its old bossy self again—"well, if I did, I've got some news for you. A person HAS a pet. An animal IS a pet. A person can't be an animal's pet, E V E R . "

"And I have some news for you,"
the brontosaurus said to Lulu, except that
he spoke more politely than Lulu
had done. "You're about to be the first
person—ever—to be an animal's pet.
Congratulations and, once again, happy
birthday."

He reached out a hand (or whatever you
want to call it) and gently scooped Lulu
off the forest floor.

He then plunked her gently down where his back met his neck. "Hold on tight, little pet," he said to Lulu. "I'll pull off some leaves from the tops of the trees for your breakfast. And then I'm taking you home to live with me."

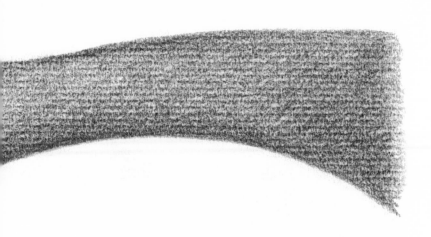

"No!" yelled Lulu. "No! No! No! A billion zillion times no."

"Yes, yes, yes," the brontosaurus replied. "I'll feed you and pat you and play with you and treat you very nicely. And all I'll expect from you is to sit and roll over and fetch a ball and do cute tricks." (What did he think she was, some kind of dog-girl? I really don't know; I can't read a dinosaur's mind.)

Lulu thought about screeching and throwing herself on the forest floor, except that the forest floor was a long way down. She thought about squeezing the dinosaur dead, except that she needed both hands to hang on to his neck. She thought about swinging and swinging her suitcase and bonking him on the head, except that she'd left her suitcase under a tree. And she couldn't stomp on his foot, because his feet were far too far from his back, where he'd plunked her.

Then Lulu started to think that the only thing farther from where the brontosaurus had plunked her was her home, her home where her mom and her dad were waiting, her very own home where no one—not even when she was being a pain (which was most of the time)—had ever, ever expected her to sit and roll over and fetch and do cute tricks.

"I want to go home to *my* house," Lulu told the brontosaurus, then added in a lot-less-bossier voice, "Please let me go back to my house, Mr. B."

This was maybe the very first time in Lulu's entire life that she, without being told, had used the P word. And yet the brontosaurus shook his head no. "Once you get used to it," he kindly told Lulu, "I truly believe that you'll like being a pet."

Lulu imagined being a pet in the house of this brontosaurus and never seeing her mom or her dad again. She imagined eating leaves and doing cute tricks. And she said to herself that if only she could turn today into yesterday, she wouldn't go looking for dinosaurs in the forest and she wouldn't say, "Foo on you" to her mom and her dad.

She was feeling especially sorry that she had ever said, "Foo on you" to her mom and her dad.

chapter eleven

The brontosaurus pulled leaves off the trees and was offering them to Lulu. She grabbed them and threw them angrily away.

"A simple 'no, thank you' will do," the brontosaurus said to Lulu. "And I really liked that 'please' you used before."

"So please please please, let me please go home!" yelled Lulu.

"Your yelling is hurting my ears," said the dinosaur. "But I have to admit that even if you had asked me softly and sweetly, I still would want to keep you here with me. I've been lonely, and a pet is a very good thing."

For hours and hours and hours, from early morning till just past noon, Lulu kept telling the brontosaurus he had to let her go home, and the brontosaurus kept telling Lulu no. He also kept assuring her that he'd do his absolute best to make her happy. He spoke in such a kind and nice and polite and patient voice that after a while Lulu was talking, not yelling. And after a while she was talking softly and sweetly. And pretty soon after that, she started to cry.

Yes, Lulu started to cry. And it wasn't very often that Lulu cried. She'd rather screech till the lightbulbs burst and all of that other stuff, but right now she didn't feel screechy—she felt teary. And so she cried and cried and cried, soaking the brontosaurus with her tears.

He patiently waited as Lulu continued soaking him, and the forest floor, with her tears. He patiently waited some more and then he said, "I'm sorry I'm making you cry, little pet, but I won't be changing my mind. Would you like a tissue?"

Lulu now understood that no matter how hard she cried and how nice this dinosaur was, he was determined to keep her as his pet. And she now understood that if she was determined to NOT be his pet, she would have to escape. She cried just a little bit longer, but while she was crying on the outside, she was—on the inside—making a getaway plan.

Sniffing a watery sniff, Lulu said to the brontosaurus, "Thank you, Mr. B, I do need some tissues. If you'll just let me down on the forest floor for a minute, I'm sure I can find a box of them in my suitcase."

The brontosaurus lowered his head and his neck to the floor of the forest. Lulu slid off, stood up, and smiled a small smile. She walked to her suitcase, opened it, poked around for a while, and found (are you surprised?) a big box of tissues.

But instead of taking the tissues out,
she put her sleeping bag in, snapped her
suitcase shut, and . . . started running.

The brontosaurus stood stiff and still,
as if he'd been glued to the ground.
And then he started running after Lulu.
But Lulu had darted off the path, into
the heart of the forest, into a part of
the forest where the trees grew so close
together that a creature as huge as this
dinosaur could not fit. She zigged and she
zagged and she zigged and she zagged
through those close-together trees while
the brontosaurus looked for spaces to
squeeze through.

He was trying his hardest to catch her—as hard as a mountain-size creature can try—but she was leaving him farther and farther behind. "Come back, little pet, come back," Lulu could hear him calling, first loudly, then softer and softer. "Come back, little pet. I know you'll be happy with me."

"Come back, little pet. . . ." His voice grew ever softer. And soon she could not hear his voice anymore.

Since Lulu could not hear his voice anymore, she stopped running and started walking. She tromped through the forest in silence, heading for home.

But she wasn't swinging her suitcase
and she wasn't singing her song, and
although she very much wanted to see her
mom and her dad again, and very much
wanted NOT to be a pet, she felt kind of
bad about the brontosaurus.
(And so do I. Because even though I'm
the person writing this story, I don't
like leaving him all alone, sadly calling,
"Come back, little pet. Come back.")

chapter twelve

But then, after maybe an hour, Lulu suddenly heard a different voice, a not-so-friendly voice, saying, "Hold it right there." And standing up on his two hind legs, and blocking her path through the forest, stood the black bear she had stomped on yesterday.

"*You* hold it right there," said Lulu, "and please"—there was that P word again—"don't keep shaking your claw-y paws at me. If I have to stomp you, I'll stomp you, but I'd really rather not stomp you. I'd rather"—she opened her suitcase and took out a jar of golden honey—"give you this if you'll please get out of my way." (What's going on with Lulu? She'd rather not *stomp* him?)

The bear took the jar of honey, opened the top, dipped in his paw, and slurpily licked it, mumbling something that sort of sounded like "Thank you." Dipping and licking and slurping, he hurried out of Lulu's path. And she continued tromping through the forest.

Until . . . another familiar, another not-too-friendly voice said, "This time I'm eating you before you bonk me." And there was the tiger, the silky, slinky tiger of yesterday, ready to pounce on her.

"Forget the eating and bonking," said Lulu, "and try on this beautiful scarf." She pulled a long, floaty, bright green scarf from her suitcase. "It matches your eyes, and I'll give it to you if you'll please get out of my way." And the tiger, happily wrapping the eye-matching scarf around her black-and-orange-striped neck, growled something that sounded like "Thank you," and slunk away. And Lulu continued tromping through the forest.

Until . . . well, what do you think she met next? A wolf? A giraffe? A lion? Don't be ridiculous. She met—of course she met; what else?—the snake, who was hissing an even nastier hiss than he'd hissed the day before and warning her, "This time *I'll* be the tighter squeezer."

Lulu, looking disgusted, told him, "Nobody's squeezing anybody. All I'm doing is getting home today." Then she reached in her suitcase and pulled out a small flowered rug and explained to the snake, "This is for you if you'll please get out of my way. A soft rug to rest on whenever you feel like resting."

The snake took the rug in his mouth and tried (at least I think he tried) to say thank you to Lulu, though it's hard to tell when a mouth is full of rug. In any case, he went slithering off wherever a snake goes slithering. And Lulu continued tromping through the forest.

chapter thirteen

It wasn't too much later that Lulu could see that she was nearly out of the forest. She was happy that soon she would be with her mom and her dad. But along with feeling happy, she was also feeling sad when she thought of the brontosaurus she'd left behind. As a matter of fact, she pictured the poor lonely dinosaur so clearly in her mind that it almost seemed he was standing there, just outside of the forest, waiting for her.

AND HE WAS!

Was Lulu shocked? You bet! "What—
what—what," she asked, "are you doing
here, Mr. B?"

"I found a shortcut," the brontosaurus
replied.

Lulu smiled a soft, sweet smile, then
shook her head and sighed. And then she
said (and even though I'm the person
writing this story, I truly don't know why
she's saying it in rhyme):

"Please try to understand, Mr. B,
That I cannot be your pet.
Even though you're the nicest
Brontosaurus I ever met.
And if you take me away with you,
I'll keep on running back home—
Every chance that I get."

(Not a bad rhyme, though
that last line's a little lumpy.)

"I already figured that out while I was waiting for you," the brontosaurus told Lulu. "I do understand that you can't be my pet. But please understand that I can't be *your* pet either."

Well, Lulu understood and the brontosaurus understood. It seemed there was only one thing left to do. So they stood there, quietly looking at each other for a moment. And then they did it.

The brontosaurus bent his long neck till his face was close to Lulu's. He kissed her gently on the cheek and said, "Happy birthday, little pet . . . and good-bye."

Lulu put her arms around the brontosaurus's neck. She kissed him gently on his nose and said, "Don't be too lonely, Mr. B . . . and good-bye."

Then she slowly walked down the road that would take her home.

Then he slowly walked down the road that would take him home.

And although Lulu and the brontosaurus remembered each other forever, they never ever saw each other again.

The
(maybe)
End

chapter thirteen

(again)

Wait! I'm really not all that sure about this ending. It may be a little too mushy, a little too sad. But since I'm the person writing this story, I'm writing another ending and you can decide which one you'd rather have:

Well, Lulu understood and the brontosaurus understood that neither of them could be the other's pet. But why should that mean that they had to say good-bye? "Come with me and I'll give you a piece of my birthday cake," said Lulu.

"I'd like that," the dinosaur said. "May I give you a ride?"

And Lulu arrived at her house, riding happily on the back of the brontosaurus.

When her mom and her dad heard the noise of a dinosaur clomping into their yard, they remembered Lulu and they remembered her birthday. Lucky for all, her cake had already been made. "Don't worry. He isn't my pet," Lulu said. "He's only going to stay here for a piece of cake and a glass of lemonade. But he's kind of a lonely guy, and I would like to invite him back for Thanksgiving dinner."

From that time on, the brontosaurus came to Lulu's house for her birthday, Thanksgiving, and the Fourth of July. And sometimes she visited his house, though (since she didn't like eating leaves) she always brought a suitcase of pickle sandwiches. On one very special birthday she not only invited her friend the brontosaurus, but also the snake and the tiger and the bear. And the brontosaurus noticed that whenever Lulu asked anyone for anything, she always said please.

The
End
(maybe)

chapter thirteen
(yet again)

Hmmm. I'm still not totally satisfied. I'm going to try once more, because I think I need to answer certain questions. Like: Were Lulu's mom and her dad worried sick when she didn't come home that night? Had they bought her a present for her birthday? Did she completely stop being a pain and turn into polite? And how did all that stuff fit into her suitcase? I'm going to answer these questions, and when I'm done you will have your choice of *three* different endings.

Well, Lulu understood and the brontosaurus understood that, though they couldn't be pets, they could be friends. So Lulu invited the brontosaurus back to her house for some birthday cake and introduced him to her mom and her dad. They hadn't been waiting and worrying and wondering where she was because they had fallen asleep sipping their tea, and they didn't open their eyes till the brontosaurus, with Lulu riding on his back, came clomp-clomp-clomping into their front yard.

They gave her a silver necklace for her birthday.

She sang them a whole new brontosaurus song:

I *didn't*, I *didn't*,
I didn't, didn't get
A bronto-bronto-bronto
Brontosaurus for a pet.
I didn't, I didn't,
I didn't, didn't get
A bronto-bronto-bronto
Brontosaurus for a pet.

"It sure looks like you've brought one home," Lulu's mom said to Lulu.

"And we still say no, you can't have one," said her dad. And both of them waited for Lulu to screech and throw herself down on the floor and kick her heels and wave her arms in the air.

Except she didn't.

"What happened to the screeching?" asked her quite astonished mom.

And her dad asked, "What about throwing yourself on the floor?"

Lulu replied, very dignified, "I'm one year older today, and I'm not doing that kid stuff anymore."

"And she says a very nice 'please,'" said the brontosaurus.

After the cake and the lemonade, the dinosaur said good-bye, but he would return for many holiday visits. Sometimes the snake and tiger and bear came too. Although she kept getting older, Lulu never turned into perfect. She still—though less and less often—sometimes screeched and forgot about "please," though she never again in her life said, "Foo on you." But she mainly wasn't a pain, and the brontosaurus was mainly not lonely anymore.

As for how all that stuff fit into Lulu's suitcase, I'm sorry to say that I don't have a clue. I am, after all, just the person who's writing this story.

The End

Join Lulu in her next raucous adventure
from Judith Viorst and Lane Smith!

From Atheneum Books for Young Readers

SINCE a kid named Fleischman is going to hang around a whole lot in these pages, I need to tell you right away that Fleischman is not his LAST name but his FIRST name. Fleischman was his mom's last name before she married his dad and changed HER name to HIS, just like other moms' last names could be

Got it? No? Well, I'm busy, and it's time to

Anderson or Kelly before THEY got married. (Some moms don't change their last names after they're married, but I really don't feel like discussing that right now.) Anyway—stay with me here—some of these used-to-be Kelly moms might decide to first-name their daughters Kelly, and some Anderson moms might first-name their sons Anderson. Or maybe they'd name their sons Kelly and daughters Anderson. And though not too many Fleischman moms decide to name their kids Fleischman, Fleischman's mom did.

---

too bad if you don't.
tell my story.

Lulu—remember Lulu?—used to always be a big pain, till she met Mr. B, a lovely brontosaurus. Now she is just a sometimes pain, and not nearly as rude as before. But unless what she wants is utterly, totally, absolutely, and no-way-José impossible, she's still a girl who wants what she wants when she wants it.

So, what is it, exactly, that our Lulu wants? Right now I'm just saying it costs a lot of money. Furthermore, her mom and her dad, who give her almost everything she asks for, said to her—with many sighs and sorries—that they couldn't afford to buy it for her and that she would HAVE TO EARN THE MONEY TO GET IT.

Lulu thought about throwing one of her famous screeching, heel-kicking, arm-waving tantrums, except that—since her last birthday—she wasn't doing that baby stuff anymore. So, instead, she tried some other ways—politer, quieter, sneakier, grown-upper ways—of changing their minds.

First try: "Why are you being so cruel to me, to your only child, to your dearest, darlingest Lulu?"

"We're not being cruel," her mom explained in an I'm-so-sorry voice. "You're still our dearest and darlingest. But we don't have the money to spend on things like that."

Second try: "I'll eat only one meal a day and also never go to the dentist, and then you can use all that money you saved to buy it for me."

"Dentists and food are much more important," Lulu's dad explained, "than this thing that you want. Which means"—and here he sighed heavily—"that if you really still want it, you're going to have to pay for it yourself."

Really still want it? Of course she really still wanted it! She was ALWAYS and FOREVER going to want it. But paying for it herself—that might be utterly and totally, plus absolutely and no-way-José, impossible. So she kept on trying to change their minds, making her saddest and maddest and baddest faces and giving her mom and her dad some unbeatable arguments. Like, "I'll move down into the basement, and you'll get the money by renting out my bedroom." Or, "You could get money by selling our car and taking the bus instead, which would also be much better for the environment." But, great as her arguments were, her mom and her dad kept saying no and sighing and sorrying. And after her sixteenth or seventeenth try, Lulu was starting to feel a little discouraged.

Last try: "So, while all the other kids are playing and laughing and having fun, I'll be the only kid my age earning money?"

"Oh, I don't know about that," said Lulu's mom. "That little Fleischman down the street is always earning money by doing helpful chores for folks in the neighborhood. So young and already such a hard-working boy!"

(Well, what do you know, here's Fleischman, and it's only Chapter One. I told you he would be hanging around a lot.)